D060192 7

Me

Papi Juan Luis, Mami Celina, my brother, Juan, and me at an amusement park

My confirmation

Me in my school uniform

Me and my brother, Juan, in front of our Christmas tree

Mami Celina, me, and my brother, Juan, at a park

To Abuelita Mercedes, Mami Celina,
and all the role-model women in my life.
–S.S.

Para Ana-Mita Betancourt, mi cuñada.
–L.D.

Turning Pages

My Life Story

Sonia Sotomayor

Illustrated by Lulu Delacre

Philomel Books

My story is a story about books—of poems and comics, of law and mystery, of science and science fiction—written both in Spanish and in English.

Even though I was born and grew up in New York City, español, Spanish, was the language we spoke at home— the language of Puerto Rico, the island where my family came from.

I struggled to learn English. Balancing two languages in my head wasn't always easy, but books made learning fun. Reading was like lighting candles, each book a flame that lit up the world around me.

What was so special about books? Do written words have a unique magic?

At each step in my life, I would put together the answer like pieces to a puzzle.

My first memory of the power of words came
from Abuelita, my beloved grandmother. Every
Saturday, my aunts and uncles and cousins would
gather for a party at her home.

After we ate dinner, the crowded little room would get quiet. Abuelita would close her eyes and recite poems written long ago about the tropical land our family had left behind. The words she spoke sent a charge through the room and sparked memories of her faraway island home.

I didn't know how to read yet, but written words, I discovered, were electrical currents that jolted feelings to life.

vuelvo a mi mundo adorado...
I return to my beloved world...

When I was seven, I got sick and was diagnosed with diabetes. I was so afraid of the big needle used to take my blood for testing at the hospital that I ran outside and hid under a parked car! I also learned that I would have to get shots every day to stay alive. All those needles were scary!

I found my courage in an unlikely place—comic books. After reading stories of regular people who had secret superpowers that could save the world, I imagined being as brave and powerful as they were. Then I learned how to give myself the shots, and in time I got used to it.

Books, it seemed, were magic potions that could fuel me with the bravery of superheroes.

I may have been inspired by Supergirl, but I still
needed to use an airplane if I wanted to fly. When we
took trips from the cold concrete streets of the Bronx
to sunny Puerto Rico, I ate fresh mangoes that had
just fallen off the trees, sipped juice straight from the
coconut, and marveled at the shimmer of tiny glowing
creatures in the bay at night. But my favorite time
was siesta at my aunt's home in Mayagüez.

At lunchtime, we feasted on rice and beans
and chicken spiced with sofrito, a delicious
mixture of tomatoes, onions, garlic and
peppers. Then, bellies stuffed full, all my
aunts and uncles and cousins would
settle down for a nap in the peaceful
quiet of a hot afternoon.

Their naptime was my reading
time. I had my trusty books to keep me
company.

Books were my loyal friends.
They made it so I never felt lonely.

When I was nine years old, my father, Papi, who had been sick for a long time, passed away. I felt sad and confused, and my home was filled with gloom. But I discovered a place where I could feel comfort.

All summer long at the nearby Parkchester Library, I walked through the aisles and touched the musty volumes until one book after another caught my eye. I read as many books as I could; I wanted to read them all.

I was lucky to have a library that was in my neighborhood, walking distance from home. For hours, I could sail away to the wondrous lands in the stories I would choose from the stacks.

The library was my harbor, and books were little boats that helped me escape sadness at home.

THE NEW YORK PUBLIC LIBRARY
CHILDREN'S TEMPORARY BORROWER'S CARD

GOOD AT THIS BRANCH ONLY

Branch PARKCHESTER Date APR 23 1963

Sonia Sotomayor

1825 Watson Ave.

Zip Code 10472

Leaving home, though, was the farthest thought from my mind the day a deliveryman rang our apartment doorbell, hauling two huge, heavy boxes.

"What's inside?" my brother, Juan, and I asked, and Mami, my mother, told us to look.

Tearing open the packing tape, we discovered an entire encyclopedia! There were twenty-four massive books, each unveiling secrets about the world—from the tiniest atoms to the tallest mountains, from the hottest deserts to the frozen tundra. Mami had created a library in our very own home!

Every time I opened a volume, I learned new words and ideas. There were miracles of life taking place in our bodies and outside in the world around us, and I started to think more about my place in it.

I felt like a deep-sea diver exploring mysterious depths. Books were my snorkel and flippers, helping me get there.

Back on land, Nancy Drew, the young girl detective hero in dozens of books, fired my imagination. Her make-believe life was so different from mine. She lived in a big house on a tree-lined street and partnered with her dad, a successful lawyer, to solve crimes.

Despite our differences, I would doze off picturing myself in Nancy's shoes. Could I figure out mysteries, too?

Books were a time machine,
inspiring me to imagine what I
would be when I grew up.

When we moved to a bigger apartment in the Bronx, our new home wasn't anything like Nancy Drew's, but Juan and I did finally get our own small rooms. It was really just one larger bedroom divided by a thin wall, but we each got to decorate our rooms. I chose wallpaper with pictures of the constellations in the sky.

I loved reading science fiction books about journeys into deep space, time travel, and encounters with aliens.

The New York Times
MEN WALK ON MOON
ASTRONAUTS LAND ON PLAIN;
COLLECT ROCKS, PLANT FLAG

New York Post
ST PHOTOS
OM MOON

LIFE
TO THE
MOON
AND
BACK

Even more amazing, real-life astronauts had just landed on the moon! They left behind a gift of words— messages of peace from the countries back on Earth. I read everything I could about the moon landing. If that was possible, then anything I could imagine was possible, too.

Books were my launchpad, blasting me straight into my dreams.

As I got older and read more, my future slowly started to take shape, like a ball of clay that you carefully sculpt into a figure with your fingers.

In high school, my teacher assigned my class a book about boys on a deserted island who went wild because there were no rules. The boys hurt each other in the chaos of a land without laws.

This book opened my eyes. I saw why we need laws and rules to feel safe, so that people have the freedom to grow and flourish. I did not yet know that I would end up working in law, as a lawyer and later as a judge, but I was learning why laws mattered.

Books were lenses, bringing into focus truths about the world around me.

He that is without sin

The Bible, a special book we studied at my Catholic high school, taught me lessons about how to treat my neighbors.

In one story, Jesus was approached by a crowd ready to punish a woman who had done wrong. Instead, Jesus challenged them, saying, "He that is without sin among you, let him first cast a stone at her." His calm, powerful words made people think. Slowly and silently, the people let her be and went home.

I learned that we shouldn't be so quick to judge people who do the wrong things. Sometimes we make mistakes that can hurt someone else, but that doesn't make us bad people. It might just mean we have to say we're sorry, put things right, and try harder.

Books were teachers, helping me sort out right from wrong.

When I started college at Princeton University, the tree-lined paths and old stone buildings looked very different from my neighborhood in the Bronx. I was excited to be there, but I was homesick, and sometimes I felt like I was drowning in everything I didn't know.

I quickly discovered the massive Firestone Library, where I could find books on everything. It was so much bigger than my neighborhood library. I would study for hours to catch up. I even improved my writing using grammar books.

Books became my life preserver,
keeping my head above water.

All that reading taught me about the farthest reaches of the planet and even about the little island closest to my heart: Puerto Rico. I read about men and women there who worked hard, but were paid very little. I read about how Puerto Rico became a part of the United States of America.

Just like in the books, my grandfather worked in a cigar factory and got sick from the dust, and my aunt spent long days stitching handkerchiefs. Like many of the Puerto Ricans who came to New York, Mami had a hard life. She studied for many years to become a nurse and was able to scrimp and save so that her kids—Juan and I—would have a brighter future.

10 HOURS TO MAKE 24 HANDKERCHIEFS FOR 24 CENTS

Reading had long taught me about the world outside, but now I was seeing in books a reflection of the lives led by my own family.

Books were mirrors of my very own universe.

When I became a lawyer, I used cases in law books to convince judges that people on trial were innocent or guilty—how they had done right and where they had gone wrong.

Just as my own family story was mirrored
in history books about Puerto Rico, I saw that
law books reflected real-life stories of people
who got into trouble but still needed to be
treated fairly in court.

Law books were maps to guide us to justice.

Justice means treating people fairly under the law. It's also the name of what I am now— Associate Justice of the Supreme Court of the United States.

As a Justice, I study the most important words in American law—the founding document of our government, the Constitution of the United States—and decide which laws agree with it. Every day I borrow from the lessons of law books of the past and write decisions and opinions that will be bound into the law books of the future.

Books are keys that unlock the wisdom of yesterday and open the door to tomorrow.

Flame. Electricity. Magic potion. Friend.

Boat. Snorkel. Time machine. Launchpad.

Lens. Teacher. Life preserver.

Mirror. Map. Key.

The written word has been all these things
to me and more for as long as I can remember.
Like flagstones on a path, every book I ever
read took me the next step I needed to go in
school and in life, even if I didn't know
exactly where the trail would lead.

Piece by piece, my puzzle came together.
Where will your journey lead you?

Timeline of My Life

June 25, 1954	My birthday in the Bronx.
~ 1960	My first trip to Puerto Rico.
1961	Diagnosed with diabetes.
1963	My Papi died.
~ 1966	Mami got us our set of encyclopedias.
1968	Graduated from Blessed Sacrament Grammar School.
1969	My family moved to Co-op City and I got my own room in our apartment.
1972	Graduated from Cardinal Spellman High School.
1976	Graduated from Princeton University.
1979	Graduated from Yale Law School.
1979	Began my work as an Assistant District Attorney in New York County.
1984	Joined the law firm of Pavia & Harcourt.
1992	Became a United States District Court Judge for the Southern District of New York.
1998	Joined as a Judge of the United States Court of Appeals for the Second Circuit.
May 26, 2009	President Barack Obama nominated me to be a United States Supreme Court Associate Justice.
August 8, 2009	I was sworn in as the 111th Justice of the Supreme Court.

I owe much to the children who taught me that hugging is important to being happy.

This book was made possible by my collaboration with Ruby Shamir, who helped conceptualize it and bring it to life. My dear friend Zara Houshmand helped to ensure my voice came through clearly.

Lulu Delacre has illustrated my words most beautifully. We share many life experiences, and she gave me her heart in her drawings.

I also deeply appreciate the assistance of Jill Santopolo, my talented editor at Penguin Random House, who ensured children would understand my thoughts.

I treasure the wise advice of Peter and Amy Bernstein of the Bernstein Literary Agency, and my lawyers, John S. Siffert and Mark A. Merriman. I am grateful to my cousin Miriam Ramirez Gonzerelli, and to my friends Ricki Seidman, Robert Katzmann, Jennifer Callahan, Lee Llambelis, Theresa Bartenope, Xavier Romeu-Matta, and Lyn Di Iorio for providing insightful comments that improved the book.

Finally, my assistants Susan Anastasi, Anh Le, and Victoria Gómez expertly organize my life to make time for a book like this.

PHILOMEL BOOKS
an imprint of Penguin Random House LLC
375 Hudson Street, New York, NY 10014

Library of Congress Cataloging-in-Publication Data
Names: Sotomayor, Sonia, 1954– author. | Delacre, Lulu, illustrator.
Title: Turning pages : my life story / Sonia Sotomayor ; illustrated by Lulu Delacre.
Description: New York : Philomel Books, 2018. | Identifiers: LCCN 2018007247 | ISBN 9780525514084 (hardback) | ISBN 9780525514114 (e-book) | Subjects: LCSH: Sotomayor, Sonia, 1954– —Juvenile literature. | Hispanic American judges—Biography—Juvenile literature. | Judges—United States—Biography—Juvenile literature. | United States. Supreme Court—Officials and employees—Biography—Juvenile literature. | BISAC: JUVENILE NONFICTION / Biography & Autobiography / Political. | JUVENILE NONFICTION / Biography & Autobiography / Women. | JUVENILE NONFICTION / People & Places / United States / Hispanic & Latino. Classification: LCC KF8745.S67 A3 2018 | DDC 347.73/2634 [B]—dc23
LC record available at https://lccn.loc.gov/2018007247

Manufactured in China by RR Donnelley Asia Printing Solutions Ltd.
ISBN 9780525514084
1 3 5 7 9 10 8 6 4 2

Edited by Jill Santopolo.   Design by Jennifer Chung.   Text set in Cantoria MT Std.
The art was done in mixed media: oil washes on primed Bristol paper with collage elements.

PHOTOS OF MY LIFE

Friends and family at Princeton University

Abuelita Mercedes, me, and my cousin Alfred

Me and other Judges of the Southern District of New York

Me when I was an assistant district attorney

My nephews, Corey and Conner, and me at their first baseball game